ILLUSIONS II

ILLUSIONS II

The Adventures of a Reluctant Student

Richard Bach

Author of *Illusions, Jonathan Livingston Seagull*

Cover design: ©2013 Anne Dunn Louque
Cover images: ©istock.com ©vectorstock.com
Interior design: www.diamondinspiration.com

ISBN 13: 978-1495345012
ISBN 10: 1495345017

BISAC: Religion / Inspirational

10 9 8 7 6 5 4 3 2 1

What the caterpillar calls the end of the world, the master calls a butterfly.

Contents

Introduction

Illusions. A book that I knew would never have a sequel. Add a word to it? Write a different story? Not possible.

I believed this until thirty-five years after it was published, until August 31, 2012.

That day, for the first time of my life, flying, fifty-eight years of an injury-free flying record, I had a little problem. It killed me for a few days and it demolished my airplane.

I was blissfully dreaming, while they helicoptered me to a hospital. They figured I was going to die, did all sorts of things to my pretty well lifeless body.

I woke up a week later in this astonishing scene: I was in a hospital! It is so easy to die, when we're over the edge of dying, knowing "death" is a lovely beautiful part of life. Painless, distressless, perfect health.

When I came out of my coma, I was told that it would take a year to get better, to learn how to speak, stand, walk, run, read, drive a car, fly my airplane. The airplane was wreckage.

I didn't know why I lived, something I promised on the other side of dying? There was no question that Puff, my seaplane, had to fly again.

My life today, it took my little crash, a near-death event, Sabryna's certainty that I would be recovered from every suggestion of injury, my meetings with *Illusions* Messiah Donald Shimoda, with my other teachers, with Puff rebuilt; for this story to be told.

There's no blessing that can't be a disaster, and no disaster that can't be a blessing.

Violent disasters, do they always become blessings? I hope so. I hope I can have my quiet little adventures, and write them, without needing to die.

—Richard Bach
December, 2013

34. The Master, having finished the tests he had chosen, left them for a lifetime beyond Earth. He found, in time, he could surpass a Messiah's life by becoming not a teacher for thousands, but a guardian angel for one, instead.

35. What he could not do for the crowds of Earth, the Master did for his friend who trusted and listened to his angel.

36. His friend loved imagining an immortal friend who suggested ideas at crossroads in the worlds of space and time.

37. When his mortal sought understanding, the Master offered ideas, spoken through coincidence, in the language of events and in the adventures of life.

38. The Master whispered stories, tests that his mortal friend thought were built of his own imagination, tales sunk in the illusions of human belief, he wrote as he saw within.

39. From the stories, beliefs changed, for his mortal. No longer a pawn the powers of others, he began to chart his own destiny, became a mirror of his highest self.

40. No longer a distant savior far away in space and time, the Master became with practice a teacher, offered sudden lessons, ideas ever more perfect for his mortal's understanding of life itself.

41. Every test, most of them, the Master designed to be a more advanced challenge for his dear mortal, eac...**uthor Richard Bach was listed in critical condition Saturday at Harborview Medical Center, with a broken back and a traumatic brain injury after a landing accident in his experimental seaplane. Bach's plane struck high-tension wires, crashed inverted, leaving the pilot unconscious in the cockpit, near fires from broken wires. The author remains in a coma to date.**

Chapter 1

God doesn't protect anyone.
Everyone's already indestructible.

THE LANDING WAS PERFECT, a word I rarely use for my flying. A few seconds before the wheels touched the land, they brushed the tops of the grass, the soft gold whispering. I don't hear the lovely sound of wheels airborne above the grass that often. It was perfect.

Just as the wheels touched the farmer's field,

though, I couldn't see. Not unconscious not-seeing, but as though someone had slammed a black plastic visor in front of my eyes.

There was no sound. The grass, the wheels, the hush of the wind…everything was still.

I'm not flying, I told myself. That's odd. I thought I was flying. This is a dream!

I didn't wake, didn't stir from sleep. I waited, patient, for the visor to lift, and go on with Part Two of my dream.

It took a long time, it seemed to me, before the darkness left.

Way in the background, the gentlest sound, song of hummingbirds, whirring low, whirring high, lifting the dreamer up and away into the music.

While the whirring faded away, the dream continued.

Visor gone, I found myself in a room way in the sky, colored like a summer afternoon. There was a window there, and I looked down through fifteen hundred feet to the ground. A gentle

scene: trees, bright emerald, fountains of leaves
under the sun, a deep-sea river blue and calm, a
bridge over it, a little town below.

A ring of children, I saw in a field near town,
some running around the circle, playing a game
I couldn't remember.

The place around me was the gondola of a
dirigible from a hundred years ago, though
I couldn't see the balloon itself. No pilots, no
controls, no one to talk with. Not a gondola. A
floating something?

On the left side of the wall was a large door, an
airline latch to lock it, and a printed sign:

Do not open this door.

I hardly needed the advice, since the place was
a long fall from the ground. It was not moving.
Not a dirigible. What kept the room in the air?

A question all at once, in my mind.

"Do you want to stay, or go back again?"

Funny, that I should be dreaming such a
question. I want to keep living, I thought.

The idea of living beyond death is certainly interesting, but there's a reason I need to go back.

What reason? I knew somehow that my dearest friend was praying for my life. Was she my wife? Why was she praying?

I'm fine, I'm not hurt, I'm dreaming! Dying is a journey for a later year, not one for now. I'd like to stay here, but I need to go back, for her sake.

The second time: *"Your choice. Would you prefer to stay, or return to your belief of living?"*

This time I thought, carefully. I've been fascinated with dying for a long time. Here's my chance to explore what this place can tell me. And this place was not the world I knew. It was an after-life, I knew. Maybe I should stay here a bit. No. I love her. I need to see her again.

"Would you care to stay?"

I didn't want to leave my life suddenly, without telling her good-bye. It was tempting to stay, but this is not dying, it's a dream. I'll wake up, please, yes. I'm sure.

That instant the room, or the gondola, disappeared, and for a half-second I saw below me a thousand file folders, each a different possibility of a lifetime, all of them vanished as I plunged into one.

I opened my eyes, woke in a hospital room. Another dream. Next I'll wake up.

I've never had a hospital dream, didn't much like hospitals. No way to find what I was doing here, but it was time to leave. I was in a bed in the hospital, surrounded by plastic vines from somewhere into my body. It felt like not a nice place to be. A monitor showing something. My wrists were tied to the railing of the bed.

What is this place? Hello, I'm awake! Vanish this dream, please!

No change. It seemed, forgive me, real.

There by the bed was the woman I knew, she was my wife? No. I loved her, I knew. She reached for me, terribly tired, but warm, loving, happy. What was her name?

"Richard! You're back!"

Nothing hurt. Why was I tied into this rig?

"Hi Sweet," I said. My voice...my words felt like a foreign language, broken syllables.

"Oh, thank you so much, dear one. Hi! You came back!" There were tears in her eyes. "You came back..." She untied my wrists.

I had no idea why I was here, why she was crying. Was my dream somehow connected with this strange place? So much I needed to find what's going on, here.

But I had to sleep, an escape from this terrible hospital. I was gone again, a smile for her, in a minute. No dreams, no understanding, feeling fine, exhausted, drifting away from waking into my coma again.

Chapter 2

Before believing, we choose what we want to believe. Then we test it for true.

WHEN I AWOKE ONCE more, the hospital again!

She was still there. "Are you OK?"

She's my wife, I thought. Can't remember her name. Not my wife. I loved her.

"I'm fine. Where are we? Except all these wires,

tubes. What's going on? What are they for? Is it time to leave?"

My voice sounded like a broken cloud, barely English.

She had not slept.

"You were hurt," she said. "You were nearly landing when the wires..."

Not true, I thought. I never saw any wires. A crash? I never saw any crash. In fifty-some years flying, I never came close to electric wires. I remembered the sound of the tires in the grass.

"Wires were right on the ground?"

"They said you hit the wires, up in the air."

"Not true. They were wrong. I was a few inches from the ground."

"OK, they got it wrong. You're alive, now, dear one." She brushed tears from her eyes.

"I was dreaming, is all. Fifteen minutes I was gone, half an hour max."

She shook her head. "It's been seven days. I waited for you here. They said you might not make it, or you might…die from the.."

"Sweet! I'm fine!"

"You have some of their heaviest drugs in you now. You had a respirator, for days, every kind of monitor, brain scans. Your heart rate was…way too high. They thought it could stop."

"Not possible! I'm in perfect health!"

She smiled, through the tears. As though she had said the words a thousand times: "You're a perfect expression of perfect Love, here and now. You will have a perfect healing. There will be no permanent injury."

It was the first time I heard what she had said to the doctors, to the nurses, to me, for a week. She'd tell me again for a year. She would tell me again and again. It would be true.

She said that I'd recover perfectly. The medical staff thought that was highly unlikely.

I knew It was true. If I had been hurt, I would recover perfectly. I hadn't been hurt!

I had a question. "Do you have a car?"

She shook her head, no. "Yes."

"Can we leave, now?"

"You're not quite ready to go, yet."

Long silence. Next question. "Can I call a cab?"

"Wait just a bit."

Questions settled on me like butterflies. What had happened? I have a charmed life. Why am I in a hospital?

I had friends who crashed airplanes, not me. Was there a crash? Why? I had no reason to hurt Puff, my little seaplane, she had no reason to hurt me. This was not my life. I made a perfect landing, no damage. What is going on?

I wondered who she was. Very close, yet not my wife!

I puzzled that, no answer. I disappeared into the coma once again. But she knew I'd come back. She knew I'd recover. Completely.

As I drifted away, she said You are a perfect expression of perfect Love, here and now. There will be no permanent injury.

*C*hapter *3*

If we want to end this lifetime higher than we began, we can expect an uphill road.

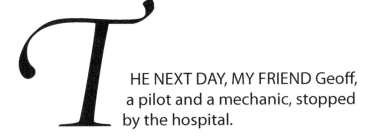

HE NEXT DAY, MY FRIEND Geoff, a pilot and a mechanic, stopped by the hospital.

"Hi, Richard. You're OK, I guess."

"I'm fine, except for all these tubes in me." My

voice was better, now, still broken. "I've got to get them out, today."

"Hope so."

"What's this about a crash? You picked Puff up? Took her home?"

"I did."

"She have any scratch, from the landing?"

He thought about that, laughed. "A scratch or two."

"What could have scratched her?" I remembered my image of landing. So smooth.

He looked at me. "Looks to me as if you hit the wires, way over the ground. The right wheel caught the wires. Things got worse after that."

"Not true. I never saw any wires, never saw any crash. I remember, before it went black. I was just skimming the grass, about to land…"

"Some other landing, maybe. Not this one, Richard. Puff was out of control from forty feet up."

20

"You're kidding."

"Don't I wish. I took pictures, afterward. When the wheel caught the wires, Puff pitched upside down, dragged a couple of power poles over, there were fires from the sparks, little fires in the dry grass. She hit the ground with her right wing, then the tail, inverted. Puff took most of the force of the crash, a couple seconds. Not much of the impact left for you."

"I think I remember..."

"I'm surprised you remember anything. It was an incredible crash."

"Nothing hurt, Geoff. I was dreaming, not flying. I couldn't see for a while, and then I was... somewhere else."

"I hope so. Was no fun being where you were, after the crash. A man pulled you out of the cockpit. Then a helicopter came, took you to the hospital. You were here thirty minutes after the crash."

"Did..." her name suddenly, "...Sabryna hear about it?"

"Yep. We flew right away, to Seattle. You were somewhere else, you stayed gone for quite a while. Some folks thought you were going to die."

"I decided not to."

"Good decision. Saw any little angels, did you?"

"Not a one, that I can remember."

"They probably figured you were OK."

"I would have liked it if they said something. *'Have a nice day…'*"

"They must have said something. You were gone for a week."

"I'll remember later."

Before he left, I said good-bye. Gone again.

Chapter 4

In every disaster, in every blessing,
ask, "Why me?"
There's a reason, of course,
there's an answer.

THE PROBLEM WITH the little rooms in hospitals is that they don't much expect that you'll be traveling. I had a narrow bed there, one with no room to move except for lying on my back awake, or lying on my back, sleeping.

I closed my eyes in the daytime, the gray of the room shifting seamless into the gray of sleep. Once in a while the dark behind my eyes was spangled with action and colors.

A dream? It was misty. A place away from the hospital? Either way, dream or far away, far away was OK with me.

The mist lifted. The field was dry hay, just been cut in the midst of a golden summer.

There was Donald Shimoda's Travel Air biplane, pure white and gold, quiet in the morning, and my little Fleet biplane. When I walked around the engine, there he was, sitting in the hay, leaning against the airplane's tire, waiting for me.

It wasn't as if there had been forty years gone… not one day had changed. Something had happened to time.

The same young karate-master as he had ever been in my mind, black hair, dark eyes, flash of his split-second smile, old memories, happening now.

"Hi, Don. What are you doing here? I thought…

you'd be far away."

"You thought there's a 'far away?'" he said. "Your belief of time and space, it separates us, does it?"

"Doesn't yours? Hasn't it been years, since…"

He laughed. "Am I separated? I hope we're not separated. Sharing your beliefs is my job." Then, "You have no idea how many angels there are, that care for you."

I smiled. "A hundred."

He shrugged. I had guessed way high. "You'd have that many if you were in trouble, to keep you from not caring for this life, if you didn't know there are tests you need to face."

"Someone in trouble, some kid in jail?"

"Dozens of angels for the kids, just trying to get through, telling them they're loved, right now."

"Not me."

"You understand. Once in a while."

"They don't talk to me."

"They do."

"Not that I recall."

He laughed, as though someone he knew was all at once standing behind me. "Don't turn around."

I didn't.

"Jonathan Livingston Seagull." A soft, gentle voice.

The same voice I heard alone while I walked in the night decades ago, I didn't know what it meant, then.

"It was you?"

I heard the voice again: "Start your pullout early."

I closed my eyes and turned behind me, laughing. "You were in my airplane, Ingolstadt, Germany, 1962. No place for you in the aircraft, but your voice behind me. I broke off the pass and barely missed the trees."

I could tell now. It was a woman's voice. "Move to the right," she said.

"Summer, 1968," I said. "Can I open my eyes?"

"Please don't."

"There was another airplane landing toward me. We missed, when I turned."

"The hand of God."

"In the desert, 1958. I was going to hit the ground. There was…"

"…an updraft. Lifted your airplane…"

"Lifted? Sheared rivets, nine something G's, blacked me out till I was in the air, safe again."

"You heard, when I spoke."

"I never understood. The desert was cold, early morning, I was going down at 350 knots in a gunnery range, I pulled up way late, knew I was going to hit the ground, and then this blackout, this explosion lifted the F-86 like a toy. I knew it couldn't be an updraft. Never knew what happened. Never heard anyone explain."

"I explained."

"I told you then! Yes, I understand the hand of God! But how did it…"

I could tell she was shaking her head. "You still don't get it, do you?"

I opened my eyes, saw an image of a lovely mist vaporizing. "When you got in trouble, we gave you a second or two to do something when you could," she said. "Once, when you couldn't, we changed space-time. The one time, call it an updraft."

"But I was thirty degrees descending," I said to where she had been. "Fifteen thousand pounds coming down at three hundred some knots, there's no updraft…"

There was a laugh. "The hand of God," she said.

"Where were you when Puff and I crashed?"

"You needed to learn about healing. There's more to learn. Puff's fine. The spirit of her is fine."

"And me?"

"You're a perfect expression of perfect Love, perfect Life, here and now."

"Do you have to be invisible?"

There was no answer.

I turned back to Shimoda.

"She said don't open your eyes," he told me.

"What is so important about closing my eyes!"

"What's so important about opening them? They tell you what's true? Even when she doesn't live in your world of space and time?"

"Well…"

"You'll see her again. Remember you wrote about a crew of angels, aboard the ship of your life?"

"Yes. A navigator, a defender, a carpenter and a sailmaker who keep the ship sailing, topmen at the crosstrees, trimming the sails, furling them in storms…"

"She's there, too. You're the commander, she's the captain's mate. You'll see her again."

Captain's mate, I thought. How I miss her now!

In the silence of the field I had time to think.
"You didn't like the Messiah-job. You told me so.
Too many people, too many expecting magic,
no one caring why. And the drama: someone
had to kill you."

"Ah, so true."

"So what's your job now?"

"Instead of crowds, I have one person. Instead of
magics, maybe there's understanding. Instead of
drama, there's...well, some. Your airplane crash
was dramatic, wouldn't you say?"

More silence. There was the crash again. Why
does he say that?

"Some of us tried Messiahing," he said.
"Nobody's made it a success. Crowds, magic,
suicide, murders. Most of us have stopped the
work. All of us, I think. We never knew there
would be so much resistance to a few simple
ideas."

"Resistance to what? What ideas?"

"Remember what she said: *You are a perfect
expression of perfect Love?*"

I nodded.

"That's one."

Sabryna, too. "Yes. I felt healed, over here, like she said. No pain, no injury, thinking's clear. But back there, in the hospital ...something happened. The airplane crash?"

There were no customers for our flights, early in the morning.

"Why you, Richard?" he said. "You believe a crash 'happened' because you have no control over events?"

Not a word about his life, what had happened for him, who he was now.

"Tell me," he said, "I'm curious. Why do you believe that you crashed your airplane."

"I didn't crash anything! They said I hit the wires, Don! I didn't see them!"

"That explains it. You're a master when things go well, you're a victim when they go out of control." He was laughing at me.

"I didn't see..." Anyone else would have said he

was crazy, not me.

"Why, I wonder," he said, "did you convince everyone you crashed?"

I was determined not to be a victim, even if I were. "For the…for the first time, Don, I had… had to fight for my life. I never had to do that."

"You will now. You know you're going to win."

I smiled at his certainty. "Right here, I'd say so. In this dream, I've already won. On the other side, something's happened. I'm not sure."

Is this a world of sides? I thought. This side I'm perfect. The mortal side, I can die?

"There are no sides," he said. "You're right. One's a dream, so's the other. There are beliefs. Here, you believe you're fine, there you'll believe you'll fight for your life. What if you can't?"

"Of course I can. I'm…I'm already perfect here and now."

"Well said."

"Nothing can hurt us, ever, can it?"

He smiled. "People die all the time."

"But they're not hurt. They come here, somewhere like this, they're perfect again."

"Of course," he said. "If they want to. Dying, the end of life, that's a belief." He frowned. "Hospitals, you don't care for. Physicians are strangers to you. Yet all of a sudden they're in your life. So what do you do with them, about them? Live, day by day, clawing your way back from your illusions of harm, to the belief of the person you thought you were. Another wrong belief. Yet it's your belief."

"You're a thought form, aren't you, Don? You're not a real image. This is a dream, the hayfield, the airplanes, the bright sunlight?"

He blinked at me, changing the talk. "Not a real image," he said. "No such thing as a real image. The only real is Love. I'm a thought-form, like you." A little smile from him. "We're living our own stories, you and me, aren't we? We give ourselves a story we think is difficult, we'll finish it now or later. Doesn't matter what others think of us, does it? It matters what we think of ourselves."

I was caught by his words. "No such thing as a

real image? No reality as thought forms, either?"

"It's all beliefs, here, too. I can change it, you can change it, whenever you want. This field, the airplanes, you can make it shift any way you wish. Earth is harder for you. Earth, you're convinced, takes time."

He lifted a hay-stem, letting it float in the air. I knew I could do that, too, in this place.

"What's true for you, Richard? What are the highest beliefs you know?"

In that place, coming as it did from almost-dying, it was easy to find what I wanted to believe. Not perfect, but a step ahead, for me.

> "Whenever we think we're hurt, we're healed in mind, first.
>
> "Holding ideas in our mind, that brings events to us, tests, rewards.
>
> "What seems to be a terrible event, is for our learning.
>
> "Others inspire us with their own adventures, we inspire them.

"We are never separated, never left by Love.

"One I got from you, Don: No mortal life is true. They're imaginations, seems-to-be, Illusions. We write and direct and star in the life in our own stories. Fiction."

The last drew me once again -- I saw a misty picture, my body unconscious on its hospital bed on Earth, the world of dear mortals there on my right, the world of after-living and its hayfield on my left. The only reality was Love, no images, no dream, just Itself.

I didn't think it was a dream when it happened. I had been flying. Something happened, before the blackness and the room in the air, and now, the meeting with Shimoda. How could it happen, how could I be in a hospital when Puff had been safe, an inch from the land?

I had a bright clear memory of what happened. Memories, my whole life, weren't they true? My airplane was already on the ground. There were no wires on the ground. Nothing could happen. Yet how could I wake in this place, or in a hospital, if nothing happened? It couldn't happen, I had such a clear image. Floating just above the grass.

"Remember what you told me?" Shimoda said. "Illusions are seems-to-be. They aren't real. You think your memories are real, but *nothing in this world is real!*"

"How can I tell if it's real?" I remembered when we flew. It wasn't forty years ago, it was now. Sunlight warming us, the airplanes, the mowed hayfield. "Are you saying this world, us planning to fly some passengers here, wherever we land, isn't real?"

"Not a bit."

The hospital was my last dream. Now I had no tubes in me, I was well and happy to be with my friend, his Travel Air, my Fleet. The hospital, was it real?

"The hospital…" he said. "It's a dream, too. Us planning to fly passengers, that's a dream. If it grows, shifts, if it's subject to time and space, even here, it's a dream. You disagree, don't you? You think that's true, the truth of airplanes, do you?"

"Don, a minute ago I thought I was in a hospital. Then I blinked and here I am awake again with you and the airplanes!"

He smiled. "So many dreams."

The smile changed me. Something was wrong.

"My airplane. It's here. But I don't own the Fleet, any more. I sold it. Years ago."

He looked a question at me. "Ready to fly?"

"No."

He nodded. "Good. Why not?"

"This is a dream, too."

"Of course it is. None of it's true, just dreams of lessons, till you let go of the school."

"The Dream School?"

The quick smile, he nodded.

The airplanes wavered, some sudden wind blurring their outline. Soon as we see something as an image, it begins to change, I thought. When I was with him before, the image of ground and water, of wrenches and vampires, all changed. Beliefs? Beliefs.

"Your memory," he said. "You had a clear image, landing?"

"Clear as anything! The sound! I heard the grass whisking on the wheels…"

"Is there any chance you thought the crash was too violent for you to see? Do you think that you might have created an image that never happened, for you to remember?"

Maybe. It's never happened before, I thought.

He took a little book from his shirt pocket, opened it. He looked at me, not at the page, and told me what the words said: *"Nobody comes to Earth to dodge problems. We come here to take 'em on."*

I hope not me, I thought. I'll dodge this problem, please. "I have to take my memories for true. Not an image, this is my memory! I was one inch from…" I blinked. "Your *Messiah's Handbook!* It's still with you?"

"You've promised to believe what you remember, even when it isn't true? This is not the Handbook. It's…" he closed the book, read

38

the title: "…*Lesser Maxims and Short Silences.*"

"Lesser Maxims? Not as powerful as the *Handbook*?"

He handed the little book to me,

> Why you and why now? Because you asked it to be this way. This disaster is the chance you prayed for, your wish come true.

I prayed for this? Nearly dying? I don't remember praying for an airplane crash. Why was this event the one I prayed for? *Why me?*

Because it was right on the edge of impossible, that's why. Because it would require absolute determination, day after week, month after month, and then it could have a host of difficulties. I needed to know whether my beliefs would overcome every one of the problems.

The doctors were required to talk about what could happen, how my life would never be the same again. I'd be required to smother every one of their beliefs with my own, beliefs I called true.

They could call on all of the knowledge of material Western medicine, I could call on what I thought was spirit, hold to it even though it didn't appear to my senses.

I am a perfect expression of perfect Love, here and now.

That mattered to me more than living in this world, this body. I didn't know that, before.

I shook my head, turned the page.

*** Unsuccessful Animal Inventions: Wolves on Stilts. ***

"*Wolves on Stilts?* How does that affect my life, Don?"

"It's a Lesser Maxim. It may not affect your life at all."

"Oh. Who wrote this odd book? You keep it in your pocket."

"You."

"M."

"You don't believe me, do you?"

"N."

"Turn to the last page."

I did. I had written an introduction, my caring for the sheep of ideas never printed, signed my name to it.

"*Wolves on stilts?*"

"You're kind," he said. "How many sheep would love to see the wolves practicing?"

I smiled. "Some. Never published? I forget."

"Maybe you'll change about forgotten memories, maybe you won't."

"I want to remember what happened to me and Puff, Don, not what my mind put in its place!"

"Interesting," he said. "Do you want to see it again, the landing as it happened in the belief you prayed for, not as you remember?"

"Yes!"

"Will you know that whatever appears to you, it isn't real?"

"*I am a perfect expression of perfect Love.*"

He smiled, nodded, one time.

and all at once, morning gone, I was aloft in a clear bright afternoon. I didn't dream it, I was flying again, Puff turning toward the farm field. I was thinking nothing but the landing. Wheels are down, flaps are down. I was a quarter-mile from the land, didn't need to see the instrument panel.

The canopy was open, I could hear the airspeed. It sounded a little fast, I moved the throttle down, a few engine revolutions. A little high, want a nice smooth landing on the grass, what a beautiful day it is, we're living a painting, aren't we, Puff?

She didn't answer. She just listened, told me through the sound of the wind, the sound of the engine, the picture of the tree tops to the left and right, the cleared space ahead on the approach.

At sixty feet above the ground, the tops of the treetops left and right were level with us, we sank softly toward the ground. The grass was mowed on the runway ahead, grown longer in the wild parts of the land around. Dry grass, the color of sunset.

I heard a quiet little ping from the right wheel, and next instant, in slow motion, the flight controls failed. Puff was all of a sudden out of control. Never happened in my life. I was no longer a pilot, I was a passenger, and Puff went down.

Do I really want to live this? I think I might better well just forget…

The electric wires scraped the steel of the right landing gear, sparks spraying a dense fireworks fountain, high voltage incandescent snow, spraying off the right side, pouring up for an instant, then turning the fountain slowly, white hot, the sound of a welder's cutting torch, over the field.

Puff tumbled, as though someone had tripped her, on her run to the land. I was tumbled, too, sudden negative high-G, a whiplash that blurred and blinded me -- all I could see was the color of blood. She was nearly upside down. In a fiftieth of a second the weight of Puff broke free from wires.

Two telephone poles were falling behind us, the wires and the sparks trailing to the ground.

Next instant, Puff was free, and she rolled. If she had a few hundred feet, she would have dropped back to level flight. a little singed but flying.

But she was free at thirty feet above the ground. She rolled to the right as hard as she could, hoping at least to keep me alive.

Then her right wing hit the ground. As though the ground was a huge spinning grindstone, the outer part of her wing disappeared.

My seat belt and the shoulder harness slammed across my chest, breaking ribs, kept my body from tumbling free from the cockpit.

The grindstone came ten feet closer, upside down, now, throwing us sidewise at five feet above the ground, stopped the propeller at three feet, then smashed the engine behind my head while it crushed us inverted, the shoulder harness broke something in my back.

Was gasoline pouring, with the gas tank over me now? The gas tank spraying over the hot engine, then exploding, would have been a flash of beautiful color.

But there was no fire in the cockpit. All at once, everything stopped. It was dead still in that scene. Nobody moving, not Puff, not me, upside down in her cockpit.

Thank you, dear Puf…

Then came the black plastic visor in front of my eyes. That was what happened. Seemed to happen. Nothing in space-time is real.

A while later, I was not with Shimoda again, but aloft in the dirigible over a different world. That wasn't true, either.

Everything in space and time is a dream.

"Let's go," Shimoda said, knowing one dream was over, time for another. No engine start, no takeoff, all at once we were flying, I was a wingman, on his right side.

He looked across the chasm between our airplanes, not a word for the dream of the crash, watching me. "Close it up a bit," he said.

Flying for a lifetime I flew first, no memories of dreams, nothing else mattered. I flew. I thought I was close in formation, five feet between the airplanes. I tucked it up to two feet from my wing to his, I could do this, with air as smooth as honey. That's about my limit. I've never touched another airplane in flight.

"A bit more," he said.

Shocked me. Closer? "You want me to touch your wing?"

"That's affirmative. Touch it, please."

I thought, for a minute, that this is a different world than the space and time on Earth. Two places here, I'll bet can occupy one space, I thought they could. He would never have asked me to touch his airplane if I was going to destroy it.

I nodded to him. Here goes. If I'm wrong I'll be leaving pieces falling back through the air behind us.

My wings slowly moved ahead, the leading

edge inches from his aileron.

The flying surfaces, the rush of air over them when I nearly touched his wings, became a suction, dragged my set of wings suddenly into the Travel Air's. They flew together all at once melted there, a foot of the wings, colors pulsing.

"Nice," he said. "This world, there's no such thing as a midair collision, do you notice? You can go ahead, it's spirits and minds, no laws of space and time here. None you can't break." He smiled. "You don't want to do this on Earth, OK?"

Reckless, I came closer, not a word spoken. My propeller spun into his wings. No rainbow-burst of fabric and wood flying into the sky. No loss of control of my plane into his. Two separate airplanes, half of them in one place.

When I slid back into clear air, my wings and his were untouched. It was not two airplanes here, but the idea of two airplanes, each one perfect, untouched by the destruction that mortals insisted when airplanes touched each other, or hit buildings, or the earth itself. You could fly your airplane through a mountain, in the after-life world, if you wanted.

Was it the same for us, too. When we're the idea of perfect expressions of love, are we untouched by collisions or accidents or disease?

"Oh," I said. "No hospitals here."

He could have said, "Nope." He didn't. "We have hospitals. Hospitals are thought-forms, dreams, for people who believe in death-by-sickness."

What a strange idea, I thought. I felt that anyone, dying out of illness, would instantly feel well when they left the world of mortals. I did, in my coma.

The two airplanes were safe. I was so used to the feeling, if I dare touch another machine in the air, we're dead! Not at all. We blend a bit, nobody's hurt.

He turned away, a steep left bank, and I pushed the power up and matched my wings' angle of bank to his.

"An idea, an expression of love, can't be destroyed," he said. "Why wasn't Puff hurt? You'll see. Her spirit's untouched, even when her body, in Earth-time, is wreckage."

I'll see it? My future? Good news! I thought it all, keeping the Fleet up with him, easing the bank down to level flight as he did, touching back the power. What a pleasure it is, flying with him!

"*You're a perfect expression of perfect Love, here and now,*" he said. "Believe it first, understand it next, your material body is healed."

"And doctors say the reason for healing is their craft," I said, "their surgeries, their medicines!"

"Sometimes they do. Sometimes they realize their own love, their own beliefs do their healings."

My body was locked in a bed in that grey concrete place in my lifelong belief of space and time. Yet we flew now over a land as beautiful as Earth's.

What a teacher, Shimoda was. Change my mind, teach me to fly my spirit-self over the beautiful lands of spirit… I'm already healed.

"I'm not your only teacher," he said.

"Oh? Tell me another."

His airplane dropped over the fields, soaring over the slopes of color. "You tell me. Every life you imagined, every one you've written, they're not fiction. You saw their spirit, writing, and when you saw, they came alive in your world. And those teachers will ever be with you."

"All my characters?"

"All yours and others that you loved."

"Bethany Ferret, Boa, Cheyenne, Stormy?"

"More."

"Jonathan Seagull?" I said. "Tink? My little Idea Fairy?"

"Of course. And Fletcher, and Connie Shak Lin and the Little Prince, Nevil Shute and Antoine de Saint-Exupery, Ray Bradbury. Think of them, ask for them, and the belief of an image will appear for you. And they'll surprise you. You know that."

Yes. Secretly. I talk with my beloved authors. "Nevil Shute and Antoine de Saint-Exupery," I said, "my friend Ray Bradbury, they're not fictional."

"Let me guess," he said. "They're living within you, aren't they? Same as you live in a few of your own readers. Do you think that you have only one life, tied with your idea of a body?"

"Oh, come on. You're kidding me."

"Am I? You're fictional, too, Richard, even though you're having a dream of life that seems non-fiction." He laughed. "Same as, you will forgive me, same as my own fictional life."

I looked at the Travel Air, floating in the air, thirty feet away. There was my teacher, once the Savior, now my friend. "Donald Shimoda," I said. "You're fictional, but you seem so real!"

"So do you."

In the middle of the land below, there was a wide runway of grass. To one side, a wooden hangar, and a J-1 Standard biplane parked. I had flown from there!

"I'm going down," I said. "I know this place!"

"Have fun," he said. "You can only land here, they say, after your life on Earth is finished. Don't know if that's true or not."

Of course he knew.

"Can I sneak down there, quiet?" I said.

"Try it if you want. Time is different here. You'll see your dog Lucky when you land, meet some old friends." He swept us together in a wide turn over the runway. "The spirits of mortals are already here, never left this place when a person decides to be born, a mortal."

Such a pretty land. He knew about a me I can't imagine, and about my dog. I so missed Lucky. He's right. I'd stay there, if ever I saw Lucky again.

Time is different? *We take only part of ourselves to Earth when we're born*? What does the other part do, while we're mortals? Suggest ideas for us to think about, write about, ways to live? Part of ourselves is our own spirit guide?

"Are you, Donald, are you...?" Too complex right now. I don't want to know. "Never mind."

"Some things for later," he said.

"I won't land," I said. "I need to see Sabryna again, finish my lifetime on earth. I owe it to her. She didn't give her consent for me to die in a crash. She prayed her affirmation: *You are a perfect expression of perfect Love, here and now.*"

"Our highest prayers, affirmations," he said. "They're Love. You know that."

His airplane vanished in the mist, or it was me who left, thinking about Earth-life.

The controls of the Fleet shimmered and dissolved, the world turned to an evening gray, the color of a hospital. I thought about what he had said, the creativity of our lifetime, our fictions come true, part of us waiting in an after-life, in heaven. Wolves on stilts.

A nurse entered, saw me smile. "Are you awake?" she said.

Chapter 5

A little time, a little perspective,
we'll see what the leveling of this site
has been making room for in our lives.

*I*T DIDN'T HURT THAT MUCH, the days in the hospital, not much that I noticed.

A lot of time for thinking, for imagining.

Why does a hospital bring sterile television into patients' rooms, when we need to meet fictional

lives linked to our own? Spirit-friends awake
in our mind, our walls of unbelief lowered for
once, when we so much need to meet them!

The characters I wrote, Shimoda said, they didn't
stop when my words stopped. Their life goes
on. I could meet them any time, in their forever-
lives, in the midst of their unwritten adventures.
They, all of them, are my teachers.

Bethany Ferret slipped into my life then, colors
flashing in my half-sleep, the bright cherry-
lemon colors of her rescue-boat's flag and her
matching crew-scarf.

What a delight, a celebration! to see her again.

She wore her duty hat, touched the cap with
her paw. "Permission to come aboard?"

Mostly solemn, that request, yet a bit of a smile
to see me again.

I laughed, silently. "Permission granted,
Captain." The bed, the images, shifted into
the bright snowcolor of her rescue boat, *J-101
Resolute*, clearing the jetty outbound, pitching
gently on the sea waves west.

I blinked at her. "I'm the guest on your boat! I should have asked your permission, coming aboard."

"You didn't know, coming from the hospital," she said. "Permission granted."

I watched the salt-colored wake, fanned wide and high astern. "This is a practice run?"

"No. A couple squirrels a half-mile off shore. They're adrift in their sailboat, halyard's parted aloft. They called for help. We'll tow them to the shore, near the forest."

"A lot of squirrels at sea?"

She smiled. "Not many."

"Mice and rats," I said, "when a human's ship goes down." I knew this, as I had written about it.

She nodded. "Plenty of those, and a few ferrets. The adventurous ones. Kits, mostly. We've never... we've rarely had to rescue an adult animal."

A voice from the interphone loudspeaker on her

bridge. "Starboard High has the squirrel's boat in sight, Captain, bearing zero one four."

She acknowledged Kimiko's voice. "Zero one four." She eased the helm a few degrees to the right. "Excuse me," Bethany said, spoke to the interphone. "Boa, a quarter ahead."

"One quarter aye."

The engines slowed, *Resolute* eased off the step, her diagonal colors waving gently at low speed.

"Forward lookout, stand by the starboard boarding ladder."

"Starboard ladder aye."

There was the little sailboat, the mainsail furled as best the two squirrels could tie it. The two were vastly relieved that a Ferret Rescue Boat had found them.

"Port High, secure the boat for towing."

"Port High, aye."

A slim ferret ran down the ladder from his post, stood by as Bethany turned her boat alongside.

"Engines idle, Boa."

"All idle, aye." The pulse of the twin screws ceased.

Bethany steered to ghost alongside the sailboat. Vincent gave the squirrels a paw to the ladder, Harley caught a line from the sailboat's forward cleat, walked it as she floated down the starboard side, belayed the line to the towing cleat.

"Line's clear the screws," Harley called.

"Boa, all ahead a quarter."

"Quarter ahead, aye." The engines dropped a few revolutions as the screws engaged, increased up a quarter.

"That's it," I said. "You go on with this long after the book about you was published."

"The book wasn't about me," she said. "It was about the Ferret Rescue Service. There was no history of them before, but you wrote, and there it was, years of service, our whole history imagined and done, when you wrote."

"Years, came true when I wrote? The book changed your past?"

"It did. Your words, your imagination, made it so. Our time, the time of invented stories, came true. May I say thank you?"

"I didn't know."

"The book is around the world, now. People who read it, now, they know the story, too. Not just us, but all the Ferret Chronicles, they have a quiet little history which can change many of us, the fiction ferrets, the mortals, too. You didn't know, did you?"

"I love the stories. I love you, all of you."

"We love you, too, Richard. Your stories told of the Ferret Code, told that there was never an evil ferret, that we live always to our highest right. Maybe that's never been done, never been written, but now it is, and nothing can erase the power of our kindness, one to another, and to humans, too."

She pressed the interphone. "Starboard High, *Resolute's* your boat. Take her ten paws from the beach by the forest, release the sailboat and crew to the shore."

"Command, aye." Down the steps like lightning on fur, Kimiko entered the bridge. "Command at your request, ma'am."

"Command aye," Bethany said, and Kimiko took the wheel from the touch of her paw, a quick glance for me.

The captain walked me down to the deck. Those stories are written love, you know that, do you?"

"Of course."

"And love is the only power in the universe. You made us real when no one had done that before. Do you know the influence you've had?"

"No. I write about adventures." I smiled for the captain. "And a little love, too."

"Go back to your mortal life, Richard. Our lives are entwined. We're your students, we're your teachers too. We will never die. Nor will you."

She took her scarf, the colors of her boat and her crew, reached it up to me, turned it around my neck.

"Bethany…"

"From the crew. From every one of us. We'll carry your love as long as we live."

I saluted the ship's flag, and the captain, a ferret custom, leaving the boat.

"Thank you, dear Bethany."

And she was gone. That moment, the *Resolute*, Harley, Kimiko, Boa, Vincent, Bethany, gone. A book. Yet for me the ferret world, and their gentle Code, lives.

How can I forget their stories?

Chapter 6

Oh, the different consciousness
   between the grieving and the dying!
One sees midnight, the other joyful
   sunrise.
One sees death, the other Life as
   never before.

I T WAS PRISON, the hospital.

How to escape? Our eyes, when they're
closed, they see differently, hear differently.

The hangar was dim, shadows and silence. There

was the wreckage of Puff, my little seaplane. All neatly laid on the concrete floor. It seemed like death: the wreckage of the right wing, struts bent and severed, the whole top of the fuselage, all of it, from the rudder to the bow, twisted, smashed, crushed from her landing inverted. Seemed like death.

I cried out, "Oh, Puff!"

A sleepy voice. "Richard?"

"Are you all right?" My voice and hers, the same words.

"I'm fine, Puff. Just a scratch or two. But it looks…that you took it all, the crash."

"No. You're looking at my mortal body. I guess I'd say 'Oh,' if I saw your body just now."

I laughed. "I'm not my body, Puff. Neither are you."

"You're OK."

"I don't remember the crash. Some said it should have killed me, except for what you did in the last two seconds."

"I did the best I could, Richard. I'm fine. Indestructible."

There she was, the image of her perfect form, perched high in the hangar, atop an engine traveler. The chain of the mortal world passing through her fuselage, no damage, of course. What a beautiful symbol for her, not a single scratch on her colors.

"I'm glad it worked. I liked having a body. This sense of danger, though, I'm not sure I liked thinking my life depended on such a delicate body, frail, here on Earth. Winds, collision, the wires. Yet there's a reason for that." Was she smiling? "I don't know what it is, but there's a reason."

What a thought. If we're spirits, indestructible, why do we bother with bodies?

"We don't have bodies, Puff. We imagine them, for the fun, for the stories, for the drama. You did, too. Your story was that you would die to protect your pilot in a crash on Earth."

A long quiet time. Her voice soft, in the silence, "I did my best. Better me than you. My wing took a lot of the impact." She was quiet for a minute, reliving. "You're done flying, too?"

"Not likely! I've flown most of this lifetime, and maybe on Earth it may take time, a bit, but I'll fly again. A few months, maybe. If I don't do it, I'll die, Puff. No point living here, if I can't fly."

She was no reason for the crash. It was not a problem for her. It was for me, not seeing the wires, and somehow needing a challenge to live.

"I'm sorry, Puff. My fault. I didn't see the wires."

"No. My fault too. I saw the wires, for a second, I thought we'd fly through. Wrong."

"You'll be rebuilt," she said. "You don't want to leave Earth yet, do you?"

"I have a mission, I think. I'll do what I have to do, rebuild my old self back. I will not live to stay on the ground!" The next words I said as though I had said them in the lost places of my memory. "You will, too, Puff. You saved my life! We'll rebuild the both of us."

"I will, too?" A flicker of hope. "You're still in the hospital, and you're thinking about rebuilding me?"

"Rebuilding us. Isn't that what the spirit requires, when we climb over the wreckage of our lives, sometimes, we go on to make our lives our own affirmation? *We are perfect expressions of perfect Love, here and now. There is no permanent injury.*"

"Really? You'll rebuild me, too?"

The suggestion that I wouldn't do it, unthinkable. Whatever I had to do, I would do, and I knew I had said that before, some meeting during the coma. I didn't remember what happened, but I had promised. If anyone told me I couldn't, today, they were part of our wreckage. We would fly again. "Yes, I will. I'm no rebuilder, Puff, but I know the man who is…"

"In Florida."

"In Florida. Valkaria, the airport where you were born in space-time."

"How…"

"I'll see him somehow. We'll truck your body, Puff, your wings, your engine, 3,000 miles to his hangar."

"I'd be… privileged… to fly with you again."

I had her promise, she had mine.

There was light and life in the hangar, so drear the hour before. The light of it brushed Puff's broken struts the color of sunshine. She would fly again.

"Thank you, Richard."

"You knew, didn't you? You were listening, at the meeting. You wondered if I would remember."

"You weren't supposed to remember."

"I don't. The certainty, though, that I would live, and you would, too, it's not an intellectual remembering, it's an emotional memory. I don't recall words, if words were used, but it was important to me, that we'd fly again."

"Just thought, not words," she said. "Some of it was…impressive."

I laughed at her solemn words. "It'll take me till I'm healed, Puff. Before then, you'll be…your body will be, off to Florida. Then three months, or four, you'll be flying again. Unless you'd prefer to vanish from Earth's sky into yours."

"Not my skies, Richard, our skies. Earth's sky is mortality, the lessons of illusions. The next sky's…a step up. I prefer to fly with you again, though, here. We have a story to finish, don't we?"

"Of course. The crash was one paragraph in our story. An important paragraph, of course. Every story loves a test, a challenge that can destroy the story. The other side, though, that's where we'll be in a little while. My body healed, yours healed, too. And we fly."

"Your choice," she said. "I'll be asleep to mortals, just broken pieces. The real me, I'll fly in spirit's sky. But when you tell me to come back here, I'll come back." She smiled, "Perfect obedience."

She thought for a minute. "I may be a little different, with my new body. Take it slowly till I remember, till I know who you are. I may be frightened. Mortals, airplanes and humans, we're slow to remember spirit."

"You as a mortal," I said, a smile. "Sure enough. We'll take it easy, for a while."

"Till then," she said.

"Do you want a different name, Puff? Something that says Determination, through this test?"

"I like my name," she said. "If I were a four-engine transport, and you were to fly me around the world...I'd still be Puff. You know what it means. So fragile, yet eternal, a perfect expression of love." She smiled. "Do you want a different name?"

I laughed. "No thank you. We shall have our same names. See you soon, Puff."

"Till then, Richard."

The colors faded, the hangar was dark again, Puff's broken pieces were still.

Her life, as mine, will continue after dying. What had Shimoda said?

In every disaster, in every blessing, ask, "Why me?" There's a reason, of course, there's an answer.

*C*hapter 7

The world of space, time and
    appearances can be wondrous
beautiful. Just don't mistake
    them for real.

*I*T WAS MIDNIGHT, nearly a thousand midnights since Lucky had died, and all at once I felt his weight on my hospital bed. I had heard of it time and again, in accounts of dear animals once gone, come to touch us again.

There was no body there just the belief of his weight, but I knew who it was.

"Hi, dear Lucky!"

Not a bark, not a sound, but I felt the familiar weight of him, I imagined him again in the dark, the soft charcoal and bronze of him, the spotless snow of his paws and his bright white scarf, always so formal.

How many times we had run across the field and meadow near our home, Lucky the Sheltie, one second half hidden in the tall grasses, then in a bound flying over the green on his next stride, running to meet me. All so beautiful now in the night, his dark eyes watching me, thoughts for words.

"Hi Richard. Want to run?"

"I have a little problem…"

He considered that. "I had one, too, on Earth. Not now. And you can run, now, too."

The land where I awoke then, was like my home, but not quite. It grew manicured, not the wild places I knew. As Lucky had said, I could run.

He trotted along by my left leg, as we had so many times before.

I slowed to a walk for him. The sun dappled the path, summer lights and shadows in the forest. A quiet afternoon.

"What's happened for you, Lucky? All the time you've been gone."

"Not gone," he said. "Listen: *Not gone!*"

Dying's a child's belief of location, of space and time. A friend's real for us when they're close, when we can see them, hear their voice. When they move to a different place, and silent, they're gone, they're dead.

Easy for him, he was with me when he wished, wondering why I didn't see him, touch him. Then he realized that was my belief. It will change, one day.

For now he was not sad for the limitation of my understanding. Most mortals have that problem.

"I've been always with you," he said. "You'll understand, some day."

"What was it like, Lucky, dying?"

"Different for you. You were so sad. You and Sabryna held me, and I lifted out of my body. No sorrow, no sadness. I got bigger and bigger… I was part of everything. I'm part of the air you breathe, with you always."

"Oh, Lucky. I miss you."

"You miss me when you can't see me, but I'm right here! I'm here! I'm all you loved about me, I'm the spirit, the only Lucky you loved! I am not gone, not dead, I never was! You walk every day with Maya, with Zsa-Zsa, around the meadows and with me, too!"

"Do they see you, dear Lucky?"

"Sometimes Maya does. She barks at me, when Zsa-Zsa sees an empty room, and you don't notice."

"Why does she bark?"

"I may be partly invisible for her."

I laughed.

He looked at me as he walked. "Time for me is different from what it is for you on Earth. We're already together any time we wish, like now."

"Not in Earth time. We call them memories." I remembered. "You'd look at us, sometimes, I knew you were thinking about us all."

"I love you still."

"When you died, I found two animal communicators. One west coast, one east coast. Sent them your picture. Called them."

"What did they say?"

"Thoughtful. Solemn."

"Not solemn!" He looked down the path. "Was I solemn?"

"No. You smiled a lot, your last year. I don't think, except in that picture, you were solemn."

"I smiled when you tried to hide from me. Remember? I'd go ahead out of sight, you'd stop, hide behind a tree I couldn't see you."

"Yes. I closed my eyes. Didn't breathe."

"Of course I found you. You heard me next to you. You heard me breathing."

"That was so funny, Lucky!" I laughed out loud, in the forest.

"I always knew where you were. Didn't you know that?" Humans, he thought, not the smartest animals, but kind to dogs. "They were wrong about solemn. Did they say anything I said?"

"You talked about when you died. You left us, you said, and you got bigger and bigger."

"I was the size of the universe. I knew I was everything. Did she say that?"

"They said that you were always with us. In every breath we breathed. You were part of us."

"Close. You were part of me. It felt as though you were with me. I thought of you a lot."

"They said why you died."

"That I didn't want to be tired, and sick?"

"Yes."

"Good communicators."

"They said you weren't sad. You didn't miss us."

"I didn't have to be sad. I knew we're always together. I didn't have the sense of loss that you had." He looked up at me. "Have."

"Lucky, it was so hard to watch you die, not have a word from you since."

"I'm sorry for that. That was a mortal's limited sense of life. A mortal dog's too. Maybe I would have felt the loss if you had died and I stayed on Earth." He looked into the forest, back again. "I came back, time and again. You could never see me. But I knew you'd see me when you died. A matter of beliefs. It will be no time since that happens."

A matter of beliefs. What had happened? Has Lucky become a teacher for me?

"The end of a lifetime," he said. "We can't help but learn when we cross the Rainbow Bridge."

"That's a human's story, *The Rainbow Bridge*."

"It's a loving thought, therefore true. Other

reunions, but the Bridge, too."

"I asked if you'd come back. They said you didn't know. If you did, someone would tell us of a little puppy, from someplace south of home."

"I still don't know. You'll be moving soon. I'll have to see about your place. I need lots of room to run. This place has spoiled me." He looked up, to see if I smiled.

"I doubt I'll be moving, Lucky."

"We'll see."

"This place is your home. It's mine, too."

"No place on Earth is your home. You know that."

We walked down the trail in silence, up to the house at the top. Lucky lay down on the porch. I sat close, leaned against the six-by-six support for the roof. He put his chin on my knee.

"We're together now," I said.

He didn't move, didn't change his expression, but his eyes, so serious, looked at me sideways.

That made me laugh, as always.

I smoothed the fur of his snow-bright neck, a brief loving touch.

If Lucky says he's always with us, I thought, what does that say about his consciousness? There is no time and space. Love is everywhere. He's happy. He's learning. He cannot be hurt. He sees and knows us. He sees possible futures. He can choose to live with us again.

If it's easy for a Shetland Sheepdog, why is it so difficult for me?

The nurse flicked on the lights, moved me one way and another, began changing the sheets.

"Thank goodness you came," I said. "I was almost asleep!"

"It's two a.m.," she said sweetly. "We change the sheets at two a.m."

I needed to leave this place. If I stayed, I was going to die. I missed my dog. I wanted to die.

Chapter 8

Someday I'm going to meet a person
who never faced a test.
I'll ask, "What are you doing here?"

I T WAS SUPPOSED TO BE a time for healing, in the hospital. Too slow. I closed my eyes, shifted away.

I opened them flying. Shimoda was now my wingman, floating off to the left. Something different with their time, I thought.

"It's not fast enough," he said.

"The time?"

"The healing."

"No. Not fast enough." I climbed the Fleet a bit, circled a lovely hilltop. "I'm doing fine here, Don. I'm healed instantly here. Part of me's back on Earth, in the hospital. Can you find me there, heal me, get my life going again?"

He was quiet for a while. "So I guess you know what people wanted, when I was the Savior."

Oh, my. Of course, I knew: *Heal me. Feed me. Give me some money.*

"Sorry."

No answer.

I turned away toward the place we started, the hayfield. "Would you maybe just give me a speed course in how you heal folks? I've never asked you for the course, but my way, it's so slow."

"Your way is the way you want to heal." He moved closer, close formation. "You want me to do it for you, heal you instantly on Earth? You

82

don't have to learn anything. You'll let me do it?"

So easy: let him do it. Someone says, How did you heal from your crash? You're well! Immediately! And I tell them, I don't know, I had a Savior heal me.

"Well, no," I said. "Just some hints, so it goes faster for me, on my own."

"If I tell you hints, is the healing your work or mine? You don't need to be healed now, you need know it when you're back on Earth. You'll wait for a savior to make you well, instead of listening to your own understanding? Your understanding doesn't work?"

"No," I said. "I'll do it myself, thank you." I know how to do it. I just need practice.

"You need practice," he said.

I frowned at him, looking across the few yards between the cockpits. He smiled, innocently.

Something he knows about healing, that I don't.

What do I know about flying, I thought, that a non-flyer doesn't know? Is it the same?

I know there's a principle of aerodynamics, works in space-time. Airplanes use aerodynamics. Learn how airplanes work, how controls work, a few simple rules, flying an airplane's easy.

I know there's a principle of spirit, I thought. It works without space-time. I am subject to that principle, in spirit and in belief of body. Learn how spirit works, a few simple rules, living a perfect spiritual life is easy.

"Wires ahead," said my wingman.

Why do they use wires here? Wires not required, telephones not necessary, in a land of spirit.

"Roger the wires," I said. I'll practice flying through them. They'll be no problem.

In seconds our airplanes hit the wires, flew through them all. Nothing happened.

That's all right, I thought. No disasters here. What do I need, on earth, for an instant healing?

Practice.

Chapter 9

What'll be your biography?
"At that point, life seemed pretty
bleak. Then (insert your name) did a
surprising thing..."

*W*HEN I WAS A BOY, I'd lie
on the grass and imagine
myself to the edge of a
cloud. They were fluffy warm places. Since
my spirit was lighter than summer air, I could
stay there as long as I wished, drift where they
went, watch this place of Earth. I'd wonder what

adventures I would meet, know I would live here till it was time to find different places and times.

"Is this what happened, after the crash? I floated on a cloud?"

"Felt like it." Shimoda said. "Something like that."

"Why did it happen?" I said.

"You forgot. Want me to guess?"

"Yes."

"You wanted your life to end in chaos. You wanted it to make no sense at all, a beautiful life till a bunch of wires snagged you and killed you and wrecked your airplane. That was the end of your story, and this..."

"Wrecked my airplane? End in chaos, maybe, Makes no Sense not like me, but the wires *wreck little Puff?* Not possible!"

"I guess I'm wrong," he said. "Why do you think you hit the wires after fifty years missing them, missing other airplanes, missing the ground, missing a world of ducks, eagles, vultures, thunderstorms, lightning strikes, snowstorms, engine failures, night, icing, fog, fires…"

"I was lucky?" I said.

"You were lucky for fifty years and then your luck quit?"

"You want me to know, don't you? You think 'bad luck' won't be the answer. You think I'll not happily live with 'bad luck.'"

"Lots of people live with 'bad luck.'" he said. "Not you? Tell me why you hit the wires, nearly killed yourself. The injuries can still kill you, everyone says. You killed Puff…"

What he said woke my silent, secret mind.

"No, Donald. I didn't kill myself, *I didn't kill Puff*."

He shrugged.

"Don't you see? I've lived a charmed life," I said. "Nothing happens without a good reason for me. Never had something that put my life, and Puff's life, on the line. Never had to work hard against something that could kill me."

"So you thought you'd hit the wires, Richard, and maybe stop living?"

"I knew exactly what would happen. I'd go off and talk with my spirit friends while my body struggled with death. No dying, though I knew I could change my mind if I got tired and gave up. I wanted to fight a long difficult fight, come out a year later the winner. I wanted Puff to come back, too. She did everything to keep me alive, and that worked, what she did. Her wing took the crash…"

"A long difficult fight, isn't that exactly what's happening?"

"Well, yes."

"And when and if you fly again, your story will end?"

"One part of it, sure enough." Flying again is a lovely end for the story, from where we struggle with death, meet with spirit guides, characters of our books, strive to live again. "That's why the crash. That's why I met up against the wires, the big invisible high-voltage wires. I brushed against dying, to live again."

"And you'll write what happened?"

"Maybe. Puff took the crash step by step in the last seconds, so I could live, don't you see, till we could fly again. My challenge is not to die before the story reaches its end."

"Lots of drama, in your life. Have you considered being a Savior?"

"No. Listen." For the first time, the chaos made sense. "My job, Don, is to rebuild myself, rebuild Puff again, come back from our beliefs, rebuild while we live our worst days, her worst fears, and my own."

"That's why you're a writer? To live through these adventures?"

"That's why I might live through this whole story: life and death, and live once again. That's why I'm me, this lifetime."

"Dramatic, positive, non-fiction. You could have done it in fiction."

"Oh," I said. "I could have done it in fiction!" I thought about it. "No. Fiction, no reader would believe it happened. Non-fiction, though, they might say, 'Interesting story.'"

"You did this all for an interesting story, Richard?"

"That what mortals do. We love our stories."

Chapter 10

If we agree that the world is not what it seems, then we have an important question: What shall we do about it?

HEN I WOKE IN THE hospital again, I was alone. The place was dismal. A little concrete room, one window to see the city of Seattle. Concrete everywhere, save for a glimpse of the Sound, a few trees, and way in the distance, the airport.

Was this part of my story? So much a struggle, this place. A year from now it would be a memory, but now it was now. I wanted to build myself up again, but not with these problems with doctors and nurses.

Never lived in a little warren like this, no room to walk, if I knew how to do that. Hour after hour, day after day, a wall-clock hummed, one showed the time, which Sabryna had taught me to read.

I was like an intelligent alien, knew nothing about this world, but I picked it up fast. Couldn't stand up, didn't have the strength to do that. Didn't have the strength, thank goodness, to eat the hospital food.

My body had lost a lot of weight. I was starving without noticing. Muscles were non-existent... how had I lost so much of my body so quickly?

I had to build myself all over again, with no power to walk, if I knew how to do it, no food, no wish to learn what the hospital wanted me to do.

Yet somewhere, a spirit guide whispered that this is as bad as it could get. It didn't mention that I could die any time, from the drugs or a lack of them. It told me it was all up to me, now. I had to scrape up the will to live and do something with it.

The bed was my gravestone. The longer I laid there, the weaker I'd become, till finally it would take all my energy to die.

It didn't seem fair, that I was lying on a bed they could simply wheel into the morgue and call my case over. "Survived the crash, but the other things, complications, drugs, killed him."

Would I have done better, just lying in the field by Puff? If this was better what would have been worse?

Dying, it's peace and joy. Dying is life! I could have laid with my airplane for a few hours and won the delight of dying. Mortals have so much to learn, they think dying is some foe, the worst of ends! Not at all, the poor things. Dying is a friend, bringing us back to life once again.

I struggled, though, just as if I were a mortal. I would not be a broken one. I had to learn to eat, learn to walk, learn to think and speak. How to run again, how to do calculations in my mind, how to take off in Puff again, fly anywhere, land so softly I'd hear the grass whisking on the tires again. Before that I had to learn to drive again, awfully more difficult, more dangerous than learning to fly again.

All those essential tasks were halted in my little cell in the hospital. Some physicians, some nurses, they thought this was a quiet place for the injured. They were kind people, the ones I knew.

I needed to get out of there!

Sabryna rented a room near the hospital to care for me. Every day she talked with me, listened to my wish to go home, told me one single reality, floating free from the dream: "You are a perfect expression of perfect Love, right here, right now. There is no permanent damage."

Without her steadfast awareness of the other side from medicines, would I have died? Yes.

How could I do it, exhausted, broken, unable to sit up more than 30 degrees without a back brace, a brace that hurt more than sitting up?

I found I had diseases that one can only contract

in a hospital. It took eight lines here to list them. I wrote them, deleted them.

This person who so disliked physiology and biology that he skipped the courses in high school, was all of a sudden, boiled in the stews of a hospital.

Don't tell me about medicines, I want none of them. Yet there I was, asked to take a whole spectrum of them from those who believed in hospitals instead of spirit, and meekly I did as requested.

Three months in a hospital! I stood this, learned to stand, thought about walking, till finally my willingness to carry my hunger strikes, my unwillingness to follow their wishes, my constant request that they please let me go home, was honored. I didn't care whether letting me go home was death or life. Just let me *go!*

They gave a pass that transferred me to a hospice, as I was close to dying. They called it, "Failure to thrive."

Sabryna was outraged. "He will not die! He will have a perfect recovery! He's going home!"

One of the doctors reluctantly changed the form: "Going home."

At last! Nor more wishing to die. Lucky knew what I didn't…we'd meet soon enough.

All at once I could look out familiar windows again, the islands about me, the birds, the sky, the clouds and the stars. A rented hospital bed, in my living room, but no streets, no concrete. Around me the books, two assistants here at home, cooking, caring.

How would Donald Shimoda have healed me, if I had asked for help? Knowing his truth, it would have taken no time, instant complete healing.

What do I have to do right now? No help from my friend, no help but my highest sense of right.

I thought about death. Like anyone, I had split-seconds, near misses, but never a long-term test of my highest right, nothing that pressed against me day after day with its suggestions:

"You can't sit, you can't stand, you can't walk, you can't eat (OK, you won't eat), you can't talk, you can't think, don't you know you're helpless?

Death is so sweet, no effort, you can let go, let it take you to another world. Listen to me. Death is not a sleep, it's a new beginning."

Those are fine suggestions, when we're desperately tired. When it seems impossible, it's easiest to let a lifetime go.

Yet we shrug the suggestions away when we want to continue with a life that isn't quite finished.

What must I do, to live again?

Practice.

Practice: I see myself as perfect, every second a new image of perfection, over and over and over, second after second.

Practice: My spiritual life is perfect right now. All day, every day, perfection always in my mind, knowing how perfect I am in spirit. I am a perfect expression of perfect Love, here and now.

Practice: Choose delight, that I am already perfect, now, a perfect portrait of my spiritual self. Always, ever, perfect. Love knows me this way, I do, too.

Practice: I am not a material human being. I am a perfect expression of perfect Love.

Practice: As I know this, the perfection of my spirit will affect my belief of body, change it to a mirror of spirit, free of the limits of the world.

Practice: The body is already perfect in spirit. Earth is a world that offers beliefs of illness. I decline them. I am a perfect expression of perfect Love.

Practice: It's not the false beliefs that trouble us, it's accepting them, gives them power. I deny that power, refuse it. I am a perfect expression of perfect Love.

Practice, over and over, never changing from a recognition of perfection. When do I stop practicing? Never.

At first I walked six steps, exhausted through the last three. I am a perfect expression of perfect Love.

Next day, twenty steps: I am a perfect expression of perfect Love.

Next day, a hundred and twenty: I am a perfect expression of Love.

At first I was dizzy standing up. It dissolved with practice, with constant repetition of what I knew for truth.

I am a perfect expression of perfect Love, right here, right now. There is no permanent damage.

Balance-practice, the little swiveling platform, and a fluffy foam pillow in the corner till I could stay upright, I am a perfect expression of perfect Love, without falling.

I switched from pajamas to street clothes, in time. I am a perfect expression, set my steps to an electric treadmill.

Two hundred steps one day,

Three hundred the next.
A quarter-mile.

I began taking the Shelties, Maya and Zsa-Zsa for their walks, a half mile on a rough dirt road, sloping down, slanting up again. I am an expression of perfect Love.

A mile… a perfect expression of perfect Love.

Mile and a half. I am not separated from Love.

Two miles. I began running. I am a perfect expression.

The affirmations were real. Nothing else in the world, except my love for Sabryna, love for the Shelties.

Love is real. All else, dreams.

One after another, the medications were dropped, till at last there were none.

I am a perfect expression of perfect Love, right here, right now. There will be no permanent damage.

It wasn't the words, it was their effect on my mind. Every time I said them, or Sabryna did, I saw myself as a perfect being, and my mind accepted it for true.

I didn't care about the appearance of my physical body. I saw a different self, spiritual and perfect, over and over again.

Seeing that, feeling it, I became my perfect spirit, and the spirit did something, some byproduct in my belief of a body, that mirrored the spiritual me.

Do I know the way it works? Not a clue. Spirit lives beyond illusions, heals our belief in them.

My job is to allow its truth, to stand out of spirit's way. Is that so difficult?

*C*hapter *11*

The best we can do is live
our highest right, gracefully as we can,
and let the Principle of Coincidence
take it from there.

SEVEN MONTHS, PUFF HAD rested in the hangar, bent wings and struts alongside, the wreckage of her tail and hull a still photograph of a crash.

I went to our hangar, not to see her, but to see her body, the way some had seen mine.

It was as if a monster, giant hands fifty feet wide, had snatched her from the air, crushed her, thrown her on the ground. When she stopped moving, fires scattered in the grass, the beast lost interest, stalked away.

She was not hurt, the spirit of her. She was asleep, dreaming of flying.

Puff had done all she could, in two seconds, and she saved my life. It was my turn, now, to save hers.

A man who's built and rebuilt many little seaplanes, an expert named Jim Ratte, came not long after. A coincidence. His business is not in the northwest, it's thousands of miles south and east, in Florida.

I was glad he was here, but I was not hoping for the best. Most likely he'd say it was a pretty difficult crash, so much has been broken. Better get a new airplane.

Not a word as he looked at her body in the hangar: saw holes in her hull, the foredeck split, aft fuselage smashed, engine and propeller broken, radiator flattened, pylon crushed, a shower of pieces broken loose from the impact.

I looked into the cockpit. Through the broken plexiglass, Puff's instruments shattered, the panel was twisted, the controls frozen. The aluminum tubes of the frame were bent, one heavy piece was sheared in two, an inch from where my leg had been.

The fabric of one wing, and the tail, was wadded up, a writer's page of useless words, thrown toward a wastebasket. The canopy had shattered an inch above my head. *Why wasn't I killed?*

At last Jim spoke, in the silence of the hangar. I was steeled for what he'd say.

"I've had a lot worse than this."

I couldn't speak. He'd had rebuilt broken airplanes *a lot worse than this?*

He put his hand, gently, on the broken deck. "I can rebuild her if you want. You'll need to put everything in a closed van, broken wings and tail, of course, drive to my shop. She's not as bad as you think. We'll have her flying again, a few months, perfect shape."

For the first day since the wires, since the crash,

I was glad for Puff. By the time I had taken the test to regain my own flying license, by the time I traveled back to Florida, she'd be ready to fly, herself!

Simple. Instead of a dead end road for her, Jim Ratte all of a sudden appeared in the hangar. "I can rebuild her."

In seconds, quick as the crash, a weight lifted from my heart.

Puff and I, the way we'd promised, we'd fly!

C hapter 12

If this world is a fiction, then soon as
we discover what's fact, we've found
our power over appearances.

HAT'S GOING
ON , DON? My last
seconds of the crash,
it was a perfect landing. But now I know what
happened … my own memory, it was fiction!"

"All lifetimes are fiction, Richard."

"Are you fiction, too?"

He laughed. "The me you see, the you I see, we're all of us fiction."

"I'm not so sure…"

"Let me tell you a little story," he said. "Once, before anyone thought of time, there was a single force in all the universe. Love. It was, and it is and it will always be, the only Real, the only principle of all life. It does not change, it does not listen to anyone. You can call it God or Demon, nonexistent, cruel, or loving, it doesn't hear, it doesn't care. It is All. Period.

"When we came to appear to be," he said, "our worlds of form and fantasy, our universe shifting changing images of stardust, it did nothing. Love is the only Is, beyond space, beyond time, anywhere, everywhere."

He stopped.

I listened to the silence. "And?" I said. "What did it do?"

"Nothing."

"Go on with your story. I want to hear what happened."

"You did. The story's over."

"What about us?"

"Nothing. We're fiction. Does reality have anything to do with dreams?"

"What can we do to be real?"

"Nothing. We already are. The deepest life within us is love. There is nothing else. Reflecting that reality, we cannot die. We don't live here in the world of spacetime. Nothing does. Nothing lives, anywhere, except love."

"What's the purpose of life here?" I said.

"Where?"

"In spacetime. There's some reason for it."

"No. Reality doesn't talk with beliefs, doesn't listen. Reality does not take form, for forms are limits, and the real is All, unlimited."

"Doesn't matter," I said, "if we're good or bad?"

"No. What's good to one is bad to another. Words mean nothing to the All. It is indestructible, it is forever, it is pure Love."

"We are nothing to the…the All?"

"Our only life," he said, "is the expression of the Is, of Love. Not what we do, but love itself. You have no way of understanding this, while you live in the world of spacetime, the land of beliefs of harm and death."

"You're telling me I can die any time?"

He laughed. "The love you know, it can't die. The annoyances, the hatreds, the wish that things could be different, gone the minute you let go of the world that seems to be. Gone. What's real, what does not dissolve, that's yours forever."

"Soon as you realize you're immortal," he said, "declare the power of Love even when it seems invisible, you'll go far beyond the illusions of space and time. In all history, the one power you never lose is your power of letting go of space and time, the joy of dying that is no wicked thing, it comes in love, to everyone."

"Then, who are you? Are you an image, a friend

who's just a thought-form, comes around when I'm ready to die?"

"We're all shifting out of the belief of mortals," he said. "I'm shifting, too. "

"What do you look like? When you're not wearing your thought-form for me?

"I look like nothing. No form. Maybe a faint little sparkle of light, maybe not."

"Some day that'll be me? I'm a friend of yours, has no form?"

"Some day? How about now?"

Chapter 13

I don't pray for the Is to recognize me. I pray for me to recognize It, perfect everpresent Love, way beyond my silly beliefs.

AFTER ELEVEN MONTHS of believing the power of Love, I thought I was pretty well invulnerable from failure. I could walk, run, I felt light and healthy, didn't want to be what I was before.

My assistants, those dear souls who had helped me every day, were gone to other patients, the story of my success part of their own.

I was cooking my little meals, exercising on my own, caring for the Shelties.

Thinking back, as I did every day, I wondered. I understand there's no such thing as death, the total end of awareness. I understand we can shift from one consciousness to another, a smooth easy switch, easy as keeping, easy as losing a dream.

Why, though, did I have the event in the room/ dirigible, with no one to say a word for me? Everyone else, dying, had some kind words from the people here. Yes, someone had printed the *Please don't fall out of the door* sign. Honestly, though, I didn't need the sign. I would have welcomed a guide, explaining what I saw:

"Welcome to your dream of the after-life. I am your conductor for this ride. We wish we could have supplied an airplane for you, but considering the haste of your journey, my idea of a flying machine had to do, so we hope you've been comfortable. You will have three chances to stay here, or go back to Earth…"

someone was correcting him: "…or go back to the Earth you know. Please speak clearly for your three answers."

"Some of your tour you will not recall, as those may suggest different choices from your designed lifetime. We hope you have enjoyed your tour, and hope that you will not share it with anyone. Your tour has been solely designed for you and will not be a journey for others."

Dreams done, back now to my decisions as a mortal.

I saw my friend Dan Nickens after I had healed from the crash. He offered me a guest room in Florida, at his house and Ann's. I don't do that often. Ever. Yet meeting the tests and the obstacles two years ago, with him flying our little seaplanes coast to coast…the worst was the sharks in the Gulf of Mexico, the sands of Death Valley…that's a different story, but we were friends.

Our adventure now was to discover whether I still knew how to fly.

Dan and Jenn, his own airplane, a twin to Puff, how important they are for us! After the crash, Dan had flown the same path that Puff had flown. Almost, since the wires had been reconnected.

"No way you could have seen them," he said. "They were blocked by the sun, they were sitting up on the final approach. Your only choice was to have flown final approach the other direction, in a tailwind."

"Makes no difference," I said. "I was responsible. I was flying the airplane."

"I know. You just couldn't have seen the wires."

Dan mentioned, by the way, that Jenn had a spare set of wings and tail feathers...would Puff like to have those? She'd be welcome to them, if she did.

Amazing, I thought. Puff's right wing was mostly wreckage, her tail was smashed, an accordion crushed against the ground. Yet, the two airplanes had flown together across the country, they shared all those miles together, lakes and rivers and deserts. Now Puff was down. Jenn, her sister, offered life of her own.

For Puff's dreaming state, I accepted the gift.

I slid down into Jenn's cockpit, next day, Dan in the copilot's seat, and after ten months on the ground, I started Jenn's engine, taxied her down the ramp into the water. Wheels up as she floated, we taxied slowly while the engine warmed. Wheels up, boost pump on, flaps down, trim set. A few seconds for an engine run-up. Jenn was ready when I was.

"OK, Dan?"

"She's your airplane," he said. "Any time."

Throttle wide open, in seconds Jenn was on the step, feathers of spray flying like summer snowflakes behind her. We were flying.

Ten months on the ground, a mind of fallen memories, worried once if I could ever walk again, fly again, here was the ground falling away beneath us, worries falling, too.

For all my concern, flying was home, same as ever it has been.

It wasn't as if flying is a difficult skill, or that flyers love the challenge of the thousand tests it charms from them.

Pilots like the tests of instrument flying, aerobatic flying, soaring flying, seaplane flying, multi-engine flying, business flying, cross-country flying, airlines, formation flying, racing, homebuilts, antiques, ultralights, warplanes. Beyond each of those brings the sense that we are one in the art, touching the beauty of flight.

For all my worries, flying was home, same as ever it had been. I tried a few water landings, simple as always. A few landings on grassy runways, each one familiar. If anything, flying had become easier than it had been, months ago.

In a few weeks, I took my flying test, an hour of talk, an hour of flying. I was legal again, after the test, to fly by myself.

Why did I think it could have been difficult? The worlds we love, are they ever difficult?

Chapter 14

What would our lives be like without tests, odds against us, adventure, risk?

A FEW DAYS LATER, word from Jim Ratte, the rebuilder. It had been eleven weeks, Puff's body had been in his shop. All her wreckage had been lifted away, the broken silhouette, the shattered windshield, bent metal and fabric and fiberglass, the engine taken off for overhaul. Switches and wires had been replaced, looms of circuits had been tested, radios repaired. Puff's gift of wings from Jennifer had been finished, painted, installed.

One day after her body had been rebuilt, Puff blinked again, her engine breathing, ready to fly! She had no memory of what had happened.

That night I couldn't sleep. I saw her in a half-dream, sparkling new, her bow resting on the lakeshore sand. It was pure delight, to touch her again. No words, joy.

"She's a pretty soul, little Puff." Shimoda sat on the sand, watching the sunlights of the airplane.

"Do machines have souls, Don?" I knew she did, I had talked with her all our flying hours.

"Everything that reflects beauty, of course she has a soul."

"She's metal and fiberglass."

He smiled. "You're blood and bones."

"Are you?"

He laughed. "I'm a thought-form, remember? Everything else you invented. We invented."

"You have a soul, Donald, a spirit to express perfect Life, perfect Love. Puff didn't?"

"Spirit overlies body," he said. "Spirit heals all things."

"Heals death."

"Not required. Death is a different face of life. You saw…it's love, shifting from one lifetime to another."

He was right. Once we visit death, once we see the beauty waiting for us, our fear's gone. Used to be never a book written, of our experience with dying. Now there are shelves, waiting to be read. The beliefs, the experiences of so many others, now.

"And Puff?"

"You saw for yourself. When she crashed, her body was lifeless, like yours was almost. Yet you could talk with her. She had no pain, no distress. You didn't either, while you were out."

"I wish I could have talked with her, then."

"Ah, that belief of seven days when you think

you remember almost nothing. What could have happened then? You didn't talk with her, did you? How strange."

"Something happened. I remember, it was desperately important for me to make Puff's body ready, for her spirit to meet us again, in this world. I'd say I made a promise to her, that we would fly again."

"Notice, Richard, that you're beginning to remember. You think it's a story you invented. It may be. The meaning is for you to say."

I looked at him, a half-smile. "May I give you a word, and you can tell me a meaning?"

He looked at me, nodded.

"Valkaria."

He laughed. "You're learning your mythologies, aren't you?"

"No," I said. "What does *Valkaria* mean? I didn't pick it. No game. It means…?"

"*Valkaria* are the daughters of the Norse god, Odin. They were Valkyries. They chose which of the warriors would die in battle. The Valkyries brought them home. They'd be heroes...or heroines, living again." He smiled. "Is that what you need to know?"

I said nothing. Listening again to what he said.

"Richard?"

"Don. The place where we trucked Puff after the crash, the hangar where Jim Ratte rebuilt her to fly again, the name of the place?"

"Not a hint. Tell me."

"The name of the airport is Valkaria."

I looked again at Puff, asleep. Not a word, but she felt happy, ready to try a body again. Our story had come where we promised it would. No one would say, beside spirits and wise friends, that our story was fiction.

*C*hapter *15*

How many of us count fictional
characters, or those we've never met,
among our closest friends?
My hand's up.

THURSDAY I FLEW WITH DAN
and Jenn to Valkaria airport, we
landed and taxied to Jim's place.
Outside in the sunlight, we saw Puff again, for
the first time.

The last time I saw her, she was unloaded from

the truck, mostly wreckage. Now, one year, 3 weeks, 3 days after our crash, Puff was the same as she had been, all the days before.

As though the crash had never happened, as though Time knew the whole thing had been a mistake, disappeared every bit of the evidence that anything had happened. Jenn stopped at Jim's hangar of Valkyries, to meet the brave one, the heroine who gave her life for me, reborn again.

I touched her gently, walked slowly around her. She was asleep, covered with her cockpit cover, embroidered now, her name stitched in the color of an afternoon sky.

"Sorry," said Time, who had slipped and now recovered, this minute the error was brushed away.

I walked to her, put my head on the soft fabric of her cover, and all at once sobbed for the sadness and the joy of this moment. That she had been through so much, and I had been through it, too, and now it, the two of us both, alive again! No proof there had ever been any crash.

There was no need to grieve for Puff, I thought, for she was with me this minute, space and time had caught up with the affirmation we had said so often: *You are a perfect expression of perfect Love, here and now.*

There had never been such a time in my life: someone destroyed for certain, whether I liked it or not. It was proved time and again that Puff was dead, histories written, photos taken. Yet came this morning and all at once she was alive again, and I was, too. The wreckage was an image on film. I do not live in paper images, nor does she. Puff was here today, ready to fly!

I would have gone on, sobbing, but stopped, wiped tears away. I'll cry if I must in some private place with her, not here.

I walked again around her, tears drying. There was no pile of wreckage. Not in the hangar, not anywhere. Did not exist. Puff was here as always she had been, her body perfect, her spirit gently asleep.

She didn't speak. Could have been my imagination. I sensed a half-language from her…*Who are you? Where am I? Leave me alone!*

Puff, it's me! We're alive again, both of us!

No response, not even half-language. She's an airplane now, a machine with no recollection of her spirit, not a dream yet of what we'd lived through. Did she have a false recollection, as I had? Did she forget what she had done, to save my life?

My body had been a machine too, not remembering: *What is this room? Who are you? Where am I? Can we leave now?*

Her spirit had told me: *"Take it slowly, Richard, till I remember, till I know who you are."*

It took me a while, too. She'd be the same. Time, I can give her.

After a long saying of hello again, maybe my imaginations, it was time to leave. My friend Dan was silent.

"Time to go," I said.

He nodded, slipped into Jenn's cockpit.

For the first time, in a year, I pressed the master switch ON, the boost pump ON, the choke lever

ON, and turned the magneto switch to BOTH. How did that feel for Puff?

Like nothing. She remembered being an airplane, not a spriit. Her propeller spun at once, the engine fired, settled down, the engine instruments swinging up, oil pressure, oil temperature, tachometer humming at 2000 RPM. All of this happening, but Puff was not awake as she had been before. Seemed she was an airplane.

Her instruments were calling good news. Everything's ready.

I said goodbye to Jim, no way to tell him what he had done in our lives, how much of my spirit he had fixed with his Valkyries, while bringing Puff into sudden perfect condition. He knew. He knew.

We taxied the long taxiways to the end of the main runway. Dan lined up to the left of the centerline, Puff and me behind on the right.

Engines good, flaps down, boost pump on.

He signaled Ready to go?

I nodded.

He looked ahead, his engine coming up to full power, his airplane moving.

I did the same for Puff: full throttle, brakes off, *Here we go, Puff!*

Not a word from her, not from Shimoda, Lucky, Bethany Ferret. She surged ahead submerged us under the sound of her engine. I held a hundred feet behind Dan, in case Puff's engine quit. It didn't. She felt like a powerful new machine, everything working just as Jim had said it would.

If Puff wasn't awake, I sure was. First flights, you expect anything to happen, that's when you can expect something to fail. Nothing did. When Dan leveled at less than a thousand feet, I pulled the throttle back to cruise. The engine slowed into a soft quiet hum, barely a sound to be heard for the fields and rivers beneath us.

The wetlands of Florida stretched out ahead of us. There is so much more of wetlands in the state, than people-land here! Gradually I relaxed, everything I worried about was the opposite, just what I hoped to see.

Dan dropped down over a lake, "Wheels up," he said. He was going to splash now, I've got five minutes flying time and he suggested that we'd land on the water.

"Wheels up," I echoed, worried again. Slowed down, not thinking whether Puff would say a word, flaps down, double-check the wheels up, while the world rose up to meet us. The water was kind, in front of us, no birds, no alligators, just the water and us. Leveled inches from the water, eased the airplane slowly down. Hope nothing breaks apart, I thought, her first touch of the water.

Next sound, hull touching water, a little skip, and touched again. A storm of spray as we slowed and stopped, floating there. Dan and Jenn had landed first, watched us land.

Nothing fell off, thank you Jim. She taxied slowly, a boat on the lake. Then we were off again, two jungle birds launched into the sky.

I breathed. Everything was working as it should. She was a young Puff again, flying perfectly! Over and over, I thought of it. Puff's alive! Me, too, by the way! We're flying!

My worries wondered why Puff wasn't talking. Not to worry. She said to give her time while she gets used to consciousness again. Airplanes don't need to talk. This one used to chat with me, she would again. Patience.

An hour later we saw our home, a blue sheet of water, the wind quieter than it had been.

A gentle slide down to the water. When the spray of landing settled, when Puff stopped, I lowered her wheels and followed Jenn, touched the shore rolling up from the beach, and we were home. No problems at all, not In the air, not in the water, not on the land.

Engines idled, and in seconds the engines of the two sisters stopped. Silence.

It was quiet for a minute, and I laughed. This was an altogether new feeling. Now that I wasn't checking Puff's instruments, now that Puff had an hour and a half in the air again…everything worked! All these last months, hoping Jim could make her fly. He did. And Dan had said we'd fly together, two airplanes, this afternoon. We did.

Dan laughed, too. Something about having some impossible hopes, not possible when we hope them, yet believing, step by step, they came true. Impossible. True. Funny.

We each sat in our cockpits, a few feet away from each other. "Fantastic, Dan! Puff's flying again!"

"She's beautiful, flying. I waited, for this flight."

"Amazing. Just amazing. When a year's dream comes true…"

He slipped out of his airplane, touched Puff's wing. "What did she say, flying again with you?"

"Nothing. Not a word."

"Not a word? Odd."

"She told me…her spirit told me, months ago, that she'll need a while before she remembers who she is, and maybe talks again."

"Good," he said. "I believe in Puff."

There were things to do with her, little things. Install a yaw-string, painted anti-corrosion grease next day on all the new…

"Dan," I said then, "Jim didn't use one bolt from the old fuselage, from the wings and tail. Not one! Now I have to coat a million brand new bolts with par-al-ketone."

"Good for him," he said.

A day later, Dan and I flew our two airplanes, more water-landings, and climbing out from the lake after her last landing, Puff said,

Hi.

Not a word for the rest of that flight. Puff the spirit was right about her reborn life.

It's all there in space and time, the crash, news articles around the world, and not a story about us flying once again. No account of the first word from Puff.

That night, a dream, I flew alone with Puff, with my friend Donald Shimoda.

"Will they ever end?" I asked, "Illusions?"

"Of course. The instant we believe we're separated from Love, we're in the world of Seems-to-Be, for an instant or a billion years.

Every world, every after-world; every possibility of hells and heavens, dance to the music of our beliefs. Far as I know, beliefs play only one language: illusions. Let illusions go, beliefs vanish. Love is with you instantly, the way it's ever been."

"You're not there, one with Love?"

"Nope. I'm a spirit guide, same as you."

"Same as you? Sorry to say, Donald, I think you may be wrong. I'm a wolf practicing on stilts. I crash often."

"Maybe. What matters to mortals, is that you finished the story that was so important from the day you and Puff lived the illusion of your crash. You didn't die, Puff didn't. You survived it whole, you learned, you practiced the way our spirit changes the belief of our bodies."

"Well, I had to try it. It worked for me. Is it true for everyone?"

"No. It's not true when we're convinced that belief can't change bodies."

I thought about that. I listened to the

affirmation of my dear friend Sabryna. So many thousands of times I had said it, the last year!

Then I whispered the one sentence of my story that's forever true for you, dear reader and for me, too:

"I am a perfect expression of perfect Love, here and now."

— end —

Puff and me flying together, touching the water in wilderness Florida: 1 year, 2 months and 22 days after our near-death event.

(Photo by Dan Nickens)

Other Books by Richard Bach

Stranger to the Ground
Biplane
Nothing by Chance
Jonathan Livingston Seagull
A Gift of Wings
Illusions: The Adventures of a Reluctant Messiah
There's No Such Place as Far Away
The Bridge Across Forever
One
Running from Safety
Out of My Mind
Messiah's Handbook
Hypnotizing Maria
Curious Lives: Adventures from the Ferret Chronicles
  Rescue Ferrets at Sea
  Air Ferrets Aloft
  Rancher Ferrets on the Range
  Writer Ferrets: Chasing the Muse
  The Last War: Detective Ferrets & the Golden Deed
Thank Your Wicked Parents
Travels with Puff: A Gentle Game of Life and Death

CPSIA information can be obtained
at www.ICGtesting.com
Printed in the USA
FSOW03n2021020517
33817FS